Where Is Christmas, Jesse Bear?

Where Is Christmas, Jesse Bear?

by **Nancy White Carlstrom**
illustrated by **Bruce Degen**

Aladdin Paperbacks

New York   London   Toronto   Sydney   Singapore

OTHER BOOKS IN THE JESSE BEAR SERIES BY
NANCY WHITE CARLSTROM, ILLUSTRATED BY BRUCE DEGEN

Better Not Get Wet, Jesse Bear
Guess Who's Coming, Jesse Bear
Happy Birthday, Jesse Bear!
How Do You Say It Today, Jesse Bear?
It's About Time, Jesse Bear
Jesse Bear, What Will You Wear?
Let's Count It Out, Jesse Bear
What a Scare, Jesse Bear

First Aladdin Paperbacks edition October 2003

Text copyright © 2000 by Nancy White Carlstrom
Illustrations copyright © 2000 by Bruce Degen

ALADDIN PAPERBACKS
An imprint of Simon & Schuster
Children's Publishing Division
1230 Avenue of the Americas
New York, NY 10020

Also available in a Simon & Schuster Books for Young Readers hardcover edition.
Designed by Anahid Hamparian
The text of this book was set in 18-point Goudy.

Manufactured in China
2 4 6 8 10 9 7 5 3 1

The Library of Congress has cataloged the hardcover edition as follows:
Carlstrom, Nancy White.
Where is Christmas, Jesse Bear? / by Nancy White Carlstrom; illustrated by Bruce Degen.
p. cm.
Summary: Jesse Bear experiences the sights, smells, sounds, and activities of Christmas, from decorations and gifts to baking and caroling.
ISBN 0-689-81962-5
[1. Bears Fiction. 2. Christmas Fiction 3. Senses and sensation Fiction. 4. Stories in rhyme.]
1. Degen, Bruce, ill. II. Title. PZ8.3.C1948Wj 2000 [E]—dc21   99-22599 CIP

ISBN 0-689-86233-4 (pbk.)

Where is Christmas, Jesse Bear?
I see Christmas over there.
Marching to the door
Knock knock boom.
Come on in, Christmas,
We'll make room.

Decorations from the attic
Spilling down the stairs,
Strings of lights and snowflakes,
Garland-covered chairs.

Where is Christmas, Jesse Bear?
I touch Christmas over there.
Baubles on the branches,
Needles on the tree,
Scratchy, smooth, and prickly,
Tickling you and me.

Sticking on the stamps,
Marking off the days,
Wrapping all the gifts
For family far away.

Where is Christmas, Jesse Bear?
I smell Christmas over there.
Baking in the kitchen,
Fudge and gingerbears,
Hot, spicy apple cider
Steaming up the air.

Lemon sugar cookies,
Stars and Christmas trees,
Cinnamon and sprinkles
Decorating me!

Where is Christmas, Jesse Bear?
I hear Christmas over there.
Clanging at the shops,
Singing on the street,
Humming merry music,
Drumming with my feet.

Winding up the music box,
Playing of the chimes,
Ringing of the sleigh bells—
Jingle-jangle time.

Where is Christmas, Jesse Bear?
I know Christmas moves out there.
Shopping with the crowds,
Skating in the park,
Moving house to house
Caroling in the dark.

Prancing with the reindeer,
Grazing with the sheep,
Flying with the angel wings,
Wiggle-jiggle leap!

Where is Christmas, Jesse Bear?
I feel Christmas everywhere.
Warming up my heart,
Lighting up your face,
Joy to the world,
Peace in this place.

Shining in the candles,
Snuggling in the chair,
Snowing on the outside—
It's here, Jesse Bear!

Christmas is here!